I'M SORRY

BY GINA AND MERCER MAYER

Reader's Digest **Kids**

Westport, Connecticut

Whenever I do something wrong,
I just say, "I'm sorry."

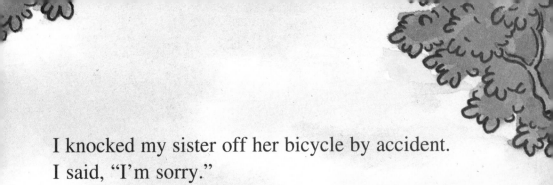

I knocked my sister off her bicycle by accident.
I said, "I'm sorry."

I left my sister's jump rope at the park.
I said, "I'm sorry."
We had to walk all the way back to get it.

I used my brother's blanket for my
Super Critter cape. It got dirty
when I was playing outside.
I said, "I'm sorry."

When I was playing hide-and-seek with my sister,
I got tangled in the curtain and pulled it down.
I said, "I'm sorry."

When I was trying to reach my favorite book,
I knocked all the other books down.
I said, "I'm sorry."
Mom helped me put them all back.

Mom said, "The baby is napping, so please play quietly."
I forgot to play quietly. I woke the baby.
I said, "I'm sorry."
Mom said, "Go play outside."

I didn't know the baby's bedroom window
was open. "I'm sorry, Mom," I said.

When I was playing football, I got tackled in Mom's garden. I said, "Sorry!"

Mom and Dad asked me to close my
bedroom window when it rained,
but I forgot. I said, "I'm sorry."

I didn't empty my pockets before
Mom washed my pants.
I said, "I'm sorry."
Mom said, "That's what you said last time."

I really wasn't sorry that I
forgot to clean my room.
I hate to do that.

But I really was sorry when I stepped in a mud puddle with my new shoes . . .

and that I didn't wash my hands before I picked up the baby's bunny.

But I was especially sorry that
I left the top off my ant farm.

At dinner Dad put some broccoli on my plate.
I said, "I'm sorry, I don't like broccoli."
Dad said, "I'm sorry, you have to
eat some anyway."

I was kind of messy when I was taking a bath. I said, "I'm sorry."
Dad made me clean up the bathroom.

After I took apart my sister's dollhouse,
I couldn't put it back together.
I said I was sorry. My sister called Mom.

While Mom fixed the dollhouse, I was supposed
to watch my little brother. Oops!

I said, "I'm sorry, Mom."
Mom said, "Sometimes saying
'I'm sorry' just isn't good
enough."

I didn't know that.

If saying "I'm sorry" isn't good enough,
I guess I'll just have to be more careful.